Emilianna

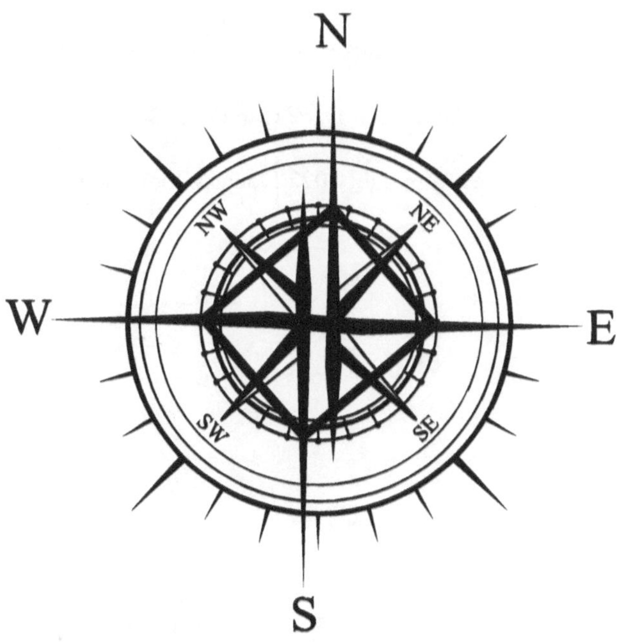

Douglas Thompson

Emilianna
by Douglas Thompson
ISBN: 978-1-913766-09-2

Cover Art by David Rix

Publication Date: October 2022

All text copyright 2022 Douglas Thompson

I
White Heron

Did I only dream
the river between us
was of blinding white light
sparkling diadems dancing
in a bright October afternoon
white heron poised with Zen patience
to catch the miracle of the eternal present
the moment that is now and never and forever?

Next day I'd say
the river was dreadful dark
and a black cormorant with red eye
had taken its place as if coated in slick oil
surveying me sceptically before spreading its
umbrella wings and taking flight as if I was the rare
interloper from Africa rarely seen prehistoric throwback
send the meteors on I so deserve my exquisite extinction.

Let us meet and follow the river
winding north again in its thrashing curves
like a restless eel who forgets the predators
and postulates and predicates a different destiny
lives only as if unseen as if the stars above are not eyes
as if there are only instances and no contrivances of you or I
and in the green suburbs and the water's hubbub finds no losses
of years or nerve, of the current of feelings only ever replenishment.

Did I only dream of Emilianna? Or was she real? If she was real, what she taught me was that nothing was real. Or if she was a dream, then she taught me that everyone was dreaming and dreaming was everything. Waking late this morning, I knew that I'd been thinking of her again, her flat down by the river Kelvin, from which the fog and ice would spread in winter at dusk and dawn like nerve gas. Her flat looked out west across the winding river, on the other side of which sat my office, or the building that held my office on its fourth floor in its swelling mansard attic like an upside-down boat.

The recession was long and bit hard. I had been put down to a three-day week. Mornings when I was not at work, I would go and call on Emilianna, climb up those unimaginably primitive stairs of her tenement, which seemed almost cave-like in their poverty and neglect, and knock on her door at the very top landing. And she would make me strong coffee and embrace me and kiss the top of my head as if she was some sort of nun or priestess blessing me with the grace of a thousand unseen goddesses. She would lead me to her couch and we would sit in each other's arms, looking westwards across the river to where the lights of my office would be coming on, the boss and his wife arriving for a day's work. And we would joke about how some other me, a parallel version, might be over there with them, also starting his day's work, unaware that his doppelgänger, a ghost version of himself, was sitting here taking stock of it all, admiring life from some standpoint outside of life, above it all, in the arms of Emilianna.

It was never my intention to fall in love with Emilianna. And how can I be sure whether I did or not, since I have already said that her very existence was in question? I am a madman after all, who writes stories, and you are an even madder man or woman, who deigns to read them. But Emilianna *was* real. I am playing with you of course. Being a married man, cheating on my wife by virtue of every time I saw Emilianna, meant that unreality, an air of fiction, surrounded how I thought of her from the start. She was a knife in my side that began a fissure, a hairline crack from my head to my toes which would ultimately split me apart, make manifest my latent schizophrenia. She had such lovely long black hair and deep black eyes, and she would go strangely quiet and still when I returned her gaze, as if cultivating an air of reverence, priming herself for some imagined leap from her soul into mine. Which usually took the form of a kiss of course, osculation, that impossible metaphor for an impossible union, that fumbling attempt to decant one human mind into another.

Why did we fascinate each other? Or was it only her inexplicable fascination for me that drew me in at first? I don't know if I have any of the answers to these questions, although in the course of this delving into memory who knows what may emerge. Her flat was incredibly untidy, it existed in a state of profound and cosmic disarray, clothes strewn everywhere across every room. In her kitchen, unwashed mugs and plates and half-consumed ingredients were everywhere. One half-expected to see flocks of stray birds delving in through the windows, breaking them if necessary and glass shards falling down, to peck at the myriad crumbs.

What on earth was I doing there? I wasn't *on* earth, when I was there, is perhaps the only answer. I was on Planet Emilianna with its own unique gravity and atmosphere. Its only other inhabitants were her two black cats, Isis and Nero, who would purr and perambulate about us, often caress and be caressed by accident and design by coming close to Emilianna and I during our embraces. A threesome, a foursome, some form of bestiality? Those are earthly perspectives but everything about the domain of Emilianna was unearthly, where other rules, or no rules, might apply.

Her living room was littered with musical instruments, guitars, six-string, twelve-string, steel-string, nylon, mandolins, banjos, violas, violins, harmonicas, penny whistles, flutes, various drums. In fact, she would often play several or all of these it seemed, in the course of a single evening or even a single song, jumping between them each manically in an attempt to accompany me in whatever song I might be performing, or attempting to perform, on one of her guitars. I used to joke that I would not have been surprised to look up during a verse or chorus to find that she had procured an Australasian didgeridoo from somewhere and was accompanying me on that.

Emilianna would go out every night, when I wasn't around, or so she told me, and perform on guitar or violin in various bands in different pubs scattered throughout the surrounding streets of her bohemian district. I told her that I envied her that free and unorthodox life, so different from the strictures of my own banal suburban existence, choked under shirt and tie, burdened down by steel-edge briefcases. We would caress each other through our clothes as we sat on her sofa, press our lips together with deranged urgency, as if trying to suck the breath from each other, to unify, or substitute and swap around our spirits. Did I want to be Emilianna? And she me? In the latter case, then it would only have been for my imagination, for the stories and poems I was able to conjure up for her so effortlessly, as if I was some mysterious magician. But Emilianna was my muse when I wrote, back then, so what I created for her, she had created herself in some sense, through me as a catalyst, as medium, as alchemical, philosopher's stone.

There was a small cupboard in the wall in Emilianna's hallway, whose wood-panelled door looked strangely ancient and which she always kept locked. Occasionally she would unlock it for me and press a red button and pull various levers, after which the gravity inside the flat would alter or be suspended altogether for a few hours. We would paw our way up walls and across ceilings while her cats slowly floated around with soporific expressions on their faces, occasionally bouncing off walls like shuttlecocks or championship swimmers reversing direction between pool laps. The flat would be filled with waves of blue light during these phases, as if the River Kelvin had risen and reclaimed its ancient floodplain. Our mouths mimed and pouted, signalling mutely to each other in the manner of prehistoric fish. Objects in Emilianna's untidy residence were all set free, floating past our faces one by one in playful nocturnal parade like children's toys. A carriage clock, a training shoe, a viola, a jar of Bolognese sauce, all singing together in a silent symphony of resplendent disorder.

When she finally went back to the cupboard and pulled the rusting stop-lever down, we would lie afterwards on the floor or on top of a wardrobe or wherever the tide had finally becalmed and washed us up, in a state of mythical exhaustion,

as if the glaciers of an ice age has scoured all our
mental mountaintops flat, left our thoughts all
jumbled up like so much rubble in a terminal
moraine.

◇

One of the songs she liked me to sing to her at
her place was Leonard Cohen's *Suzanne*. Its lyrics
were of course, somewhat apt to our situation, her
location. I even made up an altered first verse and
chorus for her once and sang it to her while her
cats looked on in disgust:

> *Emilianna takes you down*
> *To her place by the Kelvin*
> *You can hear the neds go by*
> *You can spend the night beside her*
> *And you know that she's half crazy*
> *But she'd have to be to like you*
> *And she bakes you pumpkin scones*
> *Although it isn't Halloween yet*
> *And just when you mean to tell her*
> *That you cannae sing for toffee*
> *She gets you on her wavelength*
> *And she lets the river answer*
> *That she's bought milk for your coffee.*

And you want to go busking with her
Or maybe an open-mic night
And you think maybe she'll help you
To turn your dodgy poems into songs.

I am a notorious caffeine addict and she was lactose-intolerant, so her buying milk was a more significantly selfless act than you might normally imagine. But now I find myself wondering what her cats drank then. Cats are weird. They know everything, everything, about human affairs and the meaning of the universe. You can read it all in their tired and sceptical eyes. Don't fool yourself. This isn't an illusion.

How did our attraction start? It's a strange story, strange because it involves another woman, called Connie, who I wrote a book of 52 love poems for, one for each week of the year, a journal of the seasons of love. The book was published and I did a launch and lecture about it at the City Arts Centre, and Emilianna came along and sat in the audience. She had never heard of me before (who has?) and thought the lecture would be more like a workshop on writing love songs. So she was there by accident in a sense, or so she told me when she emailed me later. My poems about Connie had moved her deeply, fascinated her even, and so began our correspondence, then in due course our clandestine meetings. Who was Connie? What happened to Connie? There we arrive at another mystery perhaps, around which so much may turn. Sometimes I think that she simply split up with me, went back to her husband, as I to my wife. Other times I seem to recall that she killed herself by jumping off a bridge. Other times I fear that perhaps I killed her, metaphorically or factually, it is hard to say. Am I a surreal adulterer and philanderer, even murderer then, or simply a serial fantasist? Must you, the reader, hate one and love the other? Why not hate them all equally, by all means: be my guest. This is my story within which only I write the rules, if there are any, and my doubt and ambiguity have a vital purpose, which over time you may come to understand. Or not.

Emilianna pretended that she didn't want to know, but did in fact want to know, who Connie really was, her real name and identity. Who it was that I could have loved so dramatically and movingly, had such an impossible and tumultuous doomed romance with. I explained over time, the background of some of the poems to her. Then we started travelling together, and I would take her to various locations to show her where certain poems were written.

When we got off a train together at Queen's Park station in the southside, we were supposed to be going to a newly opened café together, but she led me, completely unconsciously in the opposite direction down a street that she couldn't have known was the one in which Connie had lived, past the house I used to come and visit her in. How to account for this? Was she some living ghost of Connie or some fractured aspect of her, an echo, a splintered after-image? I took the opportunity to explain to her how I still felt about that street, its lingering sentimental attachment, how fraught with emotion every inch of its down-at-heel architecture had been during the short time of my affair with Connie. Emilianna nodded her head repeatedly, I could see that she instantly and completely understood everything I had to say on the topic, almost before I said it.

I took her to the cafés where Connie and I used to meet. Took the same walks, recommended the same books to read. Finally I took her to Hill 60 at the top of Queen's Park, showed her the strange unkempt path past the allotments behind it, showed her the exact place where Connie and I had fallen in love. In a few days' time I knew it would be five years to the day since that weird moment when we had fallen through what I had in retrospect come to conclude must be a gap in the space-time continuum at the location. The autumn leaves were on the ground again; all we needed was an impossibly bright November day. We got one. We rigged the site up in the early morning with strings and wires and spotlights, magnetic resonance detection equipment, a dozen cameras linked to timers and infra-red beams. I told the few passing dog-walkers that we were avant-garde film-makers. When the exact moment of commemorative anniversary came, I led Emilianna through the avenue of trees, her hand in mine, trying to match everything as recorded in Connie's photo that she took that afternoon. *What will happen, what will become of me?* Emilianna asked, wide-eyed, good-naturedly, playing along with my madness.

I don't know, I said. *Maybe we will fall in love and the whole disaster will repeat again. Or perhaps I am a serial killer and I will kill you and all this bizarre ritual is some kind of insanity, a distraction, to take us both into the necessary state of intoxication.*

You're crazy, she said. *Magnificently deranged.*

Of course our failure, in whatever bizarre enterprise we thought we were engaged in, was inevitable. The light was not quite the right colour and intensity. Clouds would pass over the sun at just the wrong moment. The colours of the leaves were not exactly the same, more or less had fallen that year from each differing tree species, because Nature is like that if you ever care to study and record it closely enough. Rainfall, hours of sunshine. Spring affects summer, affects autumn, affects all the flora and fauna differently each year. Nothing ever truly repeats on this earth, the composition our composer demands is in fact endless improvisation. His template, his bars and staves, are loose indeed.

Afterwards we laid out on her living room floor colour prints of all the photographs we took that day and made a vast patchwork quilt of it. After some persuasion she took all her clothes off and lay across the photographs naked, her long black hair strewn west towards the stern fingers of light from the window, while I carefully sketched her with charcoal on cartridge paper while listening to a crackling record of Arnold Schoenberg on her Italian grandfather's wind-up gramophone. The scene concluded when a breeze from the river blew the creaking doors of the bedroom and lounge open and Isis and Nero trotted in, weaving their way across the dazzling carpet of photographs of autumn colours towards their *mother* at whose black hair they nuzzled and mewled in order to wake her from the deep hypnotic sleep into which she had fallen.

Enflamed, in her arms on her living room couch, I told her I wanted to make love to her. No, she said, because she needed to tidy her bedroom up first. I earnestly offered to help her. It took us the next twelve weeks, on her wooden floorboards on our hands and knees in blue overalls, all day twice a week, before we got her bedroom tidy. We got terrible skelfs in unexpected places but had great fun sucking them out from under each other's skin. Under the piles of clothes and bric-a-brac we found the cryptic remains of Lord Lucan, Shergar, Malaysian Airways Flight MH370, Amelia Earhart and her Lockheed Electra, Jimmy Hoffa and the Loch Ness Monster. I had high hopes for a while that we might also find something really valuable like lost Nazi treasures such as Raphael's *Portrait of a Young Man* or *The Amber Room*, but I was too exhausted and overjoyed when our mammoth task finally came to an end to be disappointed. I fell instantly asleep on the floor and woke up 10 hours later to find she'd booked a flight to Malaga. When she returned two weeks later we found from that point forward that we could only become erotically aroused together while both wearing blue overalls and her hair tied up in an appealingly workaday bun. She devised a way to button our buttons and zip our zips together at the necessary moment. I can never enter an ironmonger store innocently for the rest of my life and the mere sight of a hammer or spanner is enough to drive me to DIY while thinking of her.

My office is a very surreal one. Of course, my life is a surreal one, but let's talk about my office. The boss's wife is French, so maybe surrealism comes easier to her than to her Albion equivalent. She has a pet African Dwarf Crocodile called Arnie which I sometimes have to take for a walk along the banks of the Kelvin in my lunchbreak. It's about four feet long, nose to tail, which isn't very *dwarf* really, come to think of it. It wears a metal-spiked and diamond-studded dog collar to which is attached a stainless steel chain. We make sure it has had its lunch first before I take it out, so that it is less tempted to snap out at, and perhaps eat, small passing terriers and Chihuahuas. Sometimes if I don't keep the chain short enough, it slopes off for a quick swim in the river shallows. You should see the watery footprints it leaves on the way back up the office stairs afterwards, hear the flip-flop sounds of its tail and claws and belly as they progress over each step. One day I dropped by Emilianna's house with Arnie, and she had to hide her cats, or rather they hid themselves rather quickly, in one of her wardrobes, while Arnie cracked open a few tins of tomato soup with his jaws on the kitchen floor before we could stop him. It's a choke collar but obviously it's not very effective on an armour-plated dinosaur.

One afternoon, I called in on Emilianna and we took a walk north and west together along the winding banks of the Kelvin. The river was in spate after recent rain; it hissed like a snake. It exists in a deep gully that it has cut for itself over millennia, down below the level of the surrounding street grid of well-to-do tenements and villas. Strolling along, we looked up to the back elevations and back garden fences and hedges above us, high above muddy cliffs and outcrops. It was as if we were dreaming, passing beneath the bored everyday of other people as if in a sleepwalking reverie. But they were the sleepwalkers of course, the enslaved ones up there on the streets, like mannequins on rails.

Some dog walkers walked by and Emilianna clutched my arm, reminding me of her major paranoia, the chink in her armour, Achilles heel (delete clichés as appropriate): *her fear of dogs*. Despite various interrogations and homemade pseudo psychoanalysis and hypnosis sessions, I never managed to uncover what previous experience or childhood trauma might have accounted for this terror in her. As I attempted to have a calming conversation with her on this topic, on a park bench on which Emilianna had temporarily paused to sit and talk, a large labradoodle leapt up on me and licked the hot interior of my left ear. I could feel Emilianna shaking at my side, but with brave restraint she managed to avoid fainting or screaming until the playful canine departed and we resumed walking again.

Shortly after this, we had another odd animal encounter. Walking further along the Kelvin walkway, when no one else was about, we spotted a heron, standing very still as herons invariably do, on a small reed-covered island in the river. *Is it real, is it a statue?* Emilianna asked. I was about to talk about his excessively patient fishing method, when to our astonishment the heron himself piped up and offered his own commentary:

Oh I'm real alright. Are you real? You're like buzzing flies to me with all your nervous jerky movements. When was the last time any of you just stopped still for a good half hour and looked at a tree blowing in the wind, or clouds crossing the sky for instance? Don't you realise that this is how to make time stop or speed up or whatever you want to do with it? Time is a pliable medium like water. Oh it has currents that can drag you down if you're not careful, I'll give you that, and torrents that can sweep you away. But once you learn to swim, to swim, to swim, too-woo, too-woo...

The end of its sentence transmuted into a suitably believable bird call, then the heron spread its huge wings and flew off, as a couple of fresh dog-walkers and joggers came trundling into view, returning us to our normal reality. Emilianna and I looked at each other in wonder.

Later on we tried out what the heron told us. Standing together in the Botanic Gardens, we looked up at an aeroplane crossing the sky above at high altitude. Winter sunset was coming on, indeed the light had departed from the ground and the gardens and the city already, but was still up there in shades of glimmering gold and pink catching the reflective underside of the aeroplane's wings and fuselage. The vapour trail it was leaving as it crossed the sky was also lighting up in a wonderful glow of pink puffs, for about six lengths of the plane behind it, but would then magically and completely vanish like candy floss encountering a human tongue, leaving behind only the glorious pale blue hemisphere of the sky. Emilianna and I stood stock-still looking up, hand-in-hand for three minutes, about the time it took for that spectacle to cross the sky from one horizon to the other, and were all the richer for it. The aeroplane seemed to us both like a metaphor for something, the passing meteor of human experience engaged in the regal fly-past we call life, the beautiful fatal burn-out in which we must all go down blazing, and only the quality and strength of our flame while we were aloft is what we will be remembered for.

That evening back at hers was when we kissed for the first time. It rained heavily that night and the next morning the Kelvin was in raging spate again. Walking to the office, I saw for the first time a rare black cormorant perched on the bridge over the river. It seemed to return my look of awe with one of jaded weariness and then flew off.

We bought crayons and cartridge paper and developed a weekly ritual of drawing each other's portraits in her front room. It wasn't a fair contest really. Her long black hair falling across her shoulders and her taste in patterned scarves always gave the compositions of which she was part more drama than those of hers with me at the centre. She was the centre of motion, a fountain of energy and form, circled by Isis and Nero, while I was like a black hole, a burnt-out singularity of stillness on the page, a shadow on the eye, the flaw in a mould or a vase where the hand of the unseen, the invisible creator has held it.

I drew you
while you drew me
tracing, following the hands
of our creator, admiring
every curve of your face
your glowing eyes
and smile brimming over
with happiness

of the pure moment
which you knew how to cherish
like our unorthodox recipe
with crazy accompaniments
a bacon roll for a Vegan
I pressed fried apple into
your laughing lips.

Afterwards
walking down Buchanan Street
side by side in blinding light
we let the stations take us
lose us in the South side
inverted landscape of lost love
romance of youth
I made it to the hill, the view
to look back at the city
laid out sublimely naked
under autumn light, knowing
under one of a thousand roofs
you worked and made
your patient music
that thrums my heart.

When Emilianna and I first played music in
public together, it was in a bohemian pub near
her flat. We tore the air apart with the strings of
our guitar and violin, with the notes of her flute
and harmonica, with our impassioned voices.
Whole tenements and sections of sky were torn
away like flayed skin in some war of the heart,

like bandages on the eternally wounded. How the sun lowered and became red and gold as it filled up like a wine glass or a grape grown to ripeness, fed fat upon our irredeemable longings. Playing music in public together for the first time, it was as if the whole city was our keyboard, our fretboard, its parks and lakes our sound-holes and echo chambers. Reaching upwards, scratching at the limits of eternity with our notes, we plucked the stars from the blue twilight sky with our hands as if they were the stops of an organ. The trains rumbled in the tunnels under our feet as if they were the pedals we pumped at, bellows through which the living breath of the city was fed into our throats. The streetlights winked and elongated in rotating lines like harpstrings, like telegraph wires, like the white-painted metal girders over Central Station, like the wires of a Victorian corset, giving way, breaking. Time bled away for a moment, the abolished trams came back on ghostly rails, we saw their electric sparks leaping across the streets whose surfaces had remembered their cobbles again. The disused tunnels thrummed beneath us with hidden excursions to lost places scattered across history. Outside the pub we were playing in, birds began to congregate and go crazy, hurling themselves against the window glass, falling down stunned to lie in twitching drifts like black snow on the pavement to dazzle passers-by. By the time we finished, packed up our instruments and left, most of the birds had recovered and were participating in vast moonlit murmurations over Great Western Road in our honour. We both felt that such tributes made human applause pale in comparison.

When Emilianna and I finally made love for the first time, she said she could hear my heart beating. I, for my part, said I could hear the trains passing underneath her flat, far below, deep underground in tunnels cut by long-dead Victorian grandfathers. She said she no longer heard them, so accustomed had she become over the years to their constant presence. My heart, her trains, interchangeable, constant, only ever derailed in grand perennial calamities. As we kissed I ran my fingers inside her, as if she herself was tunnelled. Such a short route, and yet its destination exists outside of time, an organic tunnel opening onto possible futures, new life, theoretical conceptions. The trains made her whole building shake too, infinitesimally, but this too she professed inability to sense. I noticed the curious turquoise colour she had painted her room and how she had stopped short of completing it, saying that she became uncertain towards the end whether it was really the right colour. Just like life, I joked, everyone loses faith towards the end, like

Christ on the Cross. Bloody poets, everything has to be a metaphor. *Love is man unfinished*, I quoted Paul Éluard.

Using her lipstick, I drew various lines across her naked body. The River Clyde, the River Cart, the Cathcart Circle with its train stations at Queens Park, Pollockshields West, Crosshill and Mount Florida. Hill 60, Victoria Road, the circular route of the Glasgow Underground system, her stop at Kelvinbridge, her flat, my office, the River Kelvin… The lines multiplied exponentially until the tip broke off her lipstick and we both collapsed in hopeless laughter and arousal. Her left breast was Hill 60, her nipple the flagpole, while her right breast seemed to be the hill with Greek Thomson's Holmwood house on it, to which we resolved to make a visit together the next day.

Over several months we must have visited every public park and glasshouse in Glasgow. It was something of a project of ours, as were the museums and galleries. In a way, through my book of poems about Connie and I, I had turned myself into a museum, my past love life into a museum, which Emilianna and I were constantly visiting. We had season tickets. I had a season ticket to myself. I was taxidermied like the giraffe and elephant in Kelvingrove Museum, which must have dazzled the eyes of Victorians, children particularly. I was a fabulous beast, a long-extinct creature. Museums have an affinity to stations of course, like Queen Street and Central Station. All that dirty glass overhead, permitting the passage of atmospherically muted light even, particularly perhaps, on bright autumn or winter days. The yearning glimpses of blue skies above the suffering rumble of wheels and rails. Sweet killing rhythm of the everyday.

When we took each other's clothes off it was as if we were tearing out the pages of the books of ourselves. Each white page caught fire and turned into autumn leaves, yellow, orange, red and purple. Violent conflagrations that consumed us, turned us prematurely grey in the end, reduced us to silver ashes then black dust. We became an autumn park. We undid ourselves. We had mapped the ultimate diagram of human longing, studied the mathematics of romance through obsessive forensic analysis of my failed affair with Connie. But everything pointed to violence. Something had to be done.

We had to part. What we were doing could not go on. We agreed we ought to try to stop. Emilianna could read the signs in the decaying plywood sheets that she photographed all across the city. She discovered that they're everywhere once you start looking for them. Discarded by builders, blown or torn away from boarded-up windows, the back of signs in streets or parks that have been vandalised. Plywood left out in the rain for months to be repeatedly soaked and dried will slowly begin to de-laminate, and as it does each thin layer peels away in a random pattern relative to its neighbour. It's a kind of free-form al-fresco Rorschach test, a back-hand means to psychoanalyse God himself. Emilianna had her own blog *Random Rotting Plywood* exclusively for them and their interpretation. Many of them were surprisingly beautiful works of art.

The day we finally agreed to part permanently, early December, the German street markets had arrived in town and taken over George Square and St. Enoch's Square (belly button on the lipstick body map, in which case perhaps Central Station is… well, never mind). They were like something out of a Bosch or Brueghel painting, medieval contraptions, blasphemous siege engines, windmills from hell, with rotating nativity scenes up above and stands selling sausages down below…

Christmas city
we weaved our threads
past festive windows
endless streets boxes of glimpses
of lives not lived by us untied
ribbons for the gift never given

Sunset came on prematurely
filled the parks with grey twilight
gate-crashing our own thoughts
we found the past a lost lover
scrapbook of all the loss unmourned-for
doorways painted over
where only stones remember
and our hearts what of those?

I left you in the Christmas market
amid the sights and smells and sounds
our public kiss not worthy of the interest accrued
on the loan we gave each other of ourselves
as walking away alone the busker played Elvis
I can't help falling and I remembered sitting
on the back seat of a bus outside Las Vegas
crossing an impossibly romantic desert with my wife
at night in which I have now lost my way.

In George Square, I ripped up my own book
of love poems and tossed pages into each litter bin
as I passed the laughing children and the turning wheels
this winter when we put ourselves on ice without
the frivolity of ice cream with empty hands I turned
to catch the train home jam-packed with life
around my ears the long tunnel of darkness
howled towards the moon.

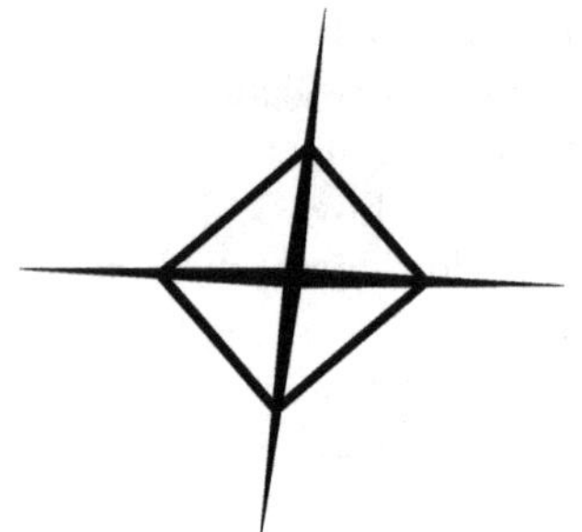

II

The Lost Spire

I needed to escape her. Emilianna. And to escape the memory of Connie too. I needed to have somewhere I could escape everyone and everything, even my wife for a while. But more than anything: escape human judgement. With some money I had inherited from my late mother, I bought a top floor corner flat in a Victorian tenement on the Gallowgate, (the name means of course: the street where they used to hang people – how appropriate that I should hang myself above it). To be alone and attempt to sort myself out, to heal myself through solitary contemplation of the confusion that other people awaken in me. From its corner turret I could see right across the city, even to the flagpole on Hill 60 in Queen's Park on the southside, where they say a Roman fort lurks long buried beneath the trees and probably Celtic remains before that, a Druid temple perhaps, strange reverberations, a Neolithic power station fuelled by human sacrifice.

I purchased a large-scale map of the city street grid and pasted it to one wall of the flat like wallpaper, and began to draw red pencil lines over it. I discovered that a perfect triangle linked Hill 60, the Gallowgate flat, and my office building, or more precisely the patch of cobbled lane just outside it, on the bend of the river Kelvin, on the way round to Emilianna's place. It was a right-angled triangle, rather than an equilateral one, which meant it could be projected into a square. The fourth point, the closing node of that square, when I drew the lines to their intersection was, I discovered to my horror, Ibrox football stadium. Or *The Cathedral of Bigotry* as I usually refer to that hateful place. The home of Scottish fascism. British Unionism, waving of the Union Jack. Scots who have been brought up to hate their own country and their own people so much as to fervently believe that Scotland cannot possibly govern itself so the English must do it for them. Imagine, if you will, if they had held a referendum in 1865 to ask all the black slaves in America whether they wanted to be free, and they had voted by a narrow majority to keep their chains because they rather liked oppression and were afraid of taking responsibility for themselves. Imagine that, and you have imagined contemporary Scotland, you hold this whole sorry mess of self-loathing and self-doubt in your hand. I recognise these psychological diseases on the national scale so well perhaps, because I have suffered from them life-long at the private level. I personify my country.

In the 2014 referendum on Scottish independence, my wife abstained. Connie and I both voted Yes. Emilianna voted No. Three women. Curious differences, curious symmetries. Red hair, brown hair, black hair. Two grown-up daughters, no children, two grown-up sons. Is Emilianna the mirror-image, the inversion of Connie? But Emilianna claimed sensible economic reasons for not voting for independence. Being a Roman Catholic by upbringing, she is no Union-Jack waver, no fan of Glasgow Rangers. Like so many Scots, she is probably secretly and deep-down a believer in independence, who is yet to be persuaded enough to transcend 300 years of programmed subservience. But let's face it: most of us get our politics from our parents, like our accents, our looks.

In Glasgow, we have to suffer 'Orange Walks' when the Unionist fascists march through the city seemingly once-a-week all summer, stopping traffic and thumping drums and playing pipes, sectarian nonsense imported from Northern Ireland, wearing ridiculous orange sashes and black bowler hats supposedly to commemorate William of Orange ('King Billy') and his victory over Irish Catholics at the Battle of Boyne in 1690. This is real life. And you think I'm surreal? One is not supposed to cross in front of, or through, an Orange Walk in progress. My father, a small but still ferocious old man by then, once tried to cross a march and was stopped by a large thug at the head of the procession, to whom my father then snarled in response: *I fought in World War Two against fascists like you.* Their sole purpose in their marches, the routes they take, is to intimidate the Catholic population of Glasgow, identifiable by Irish names and support for Glasgow Celtic. The crowds who line the streets to cheer on these parades have to be seen to be believed. Mostly over-weight with high blood-pressure, red, white and blue in the face with emphysema, belligerently ignorant, shouting slogans like *Fuck The Pope* at the top of their voices and encouraging their children, toddlers even, who they bring with them, to do likewise. They are the residual scum around the toilet pan of modern Scotland. Our equivalent of the Trumpers and Brexiteers.

This is what gathers and festers and amplifies itself weekly at Ibrox, the nexus of all evil in Scotland. A nuclear strike would probably not be enough to erase it. It is perhaps always endemic in the human character, this darkness, this foul-smelling cess-pit of sectarianism, racism, sexism, fascism, nazism. It's always with us. All we can do is keep buying toilet paper and air-freshener and keep wiping and flushing, to try to cleanse ourselves of our eternally dirty centre-points, our swirling plugholes, the open, spite-chanting mouths of these dinosaurs.

So at Gallowgate, between bouts of wallpaper-stripping and repainting, I flatter myself that I have begun to uncover the secret structure of converging ley-lines hidden underneath Glasgow. In medieval times, pilgrims used to walk along the routes of what are now Argyle Street and the Gallowgate to pray at various sacred healing wells. Some of these wells can still be found in obscure backcourts and alleyways, sidetracked by modernity and urban expansion, some built over and lost altogether, such as the one that was reputedly behind *The Saracen's Head* or *Sarry Heid*, the oldest and roughest bar in Glasgow, on the next block to my flat. Another ancient well can still be found hidden behind a certain brewery off Duke Street, at the foot of the Northern Necropolis, a hill covered in elaborate Victorian tombs. The brewery, owned by some Tory Lord, makes a popular third-rate Scottish lager traditionally pumped full of secret chemicals to make the working class vote wrong.

I researched the city archives for old black and white photographs and was amazed to discover that the Gallowgate flat had a spire over it once, right above my corner turret. A proper, properly incongruous, gothic spire, like a witch's pointy hat. It was there one presumes to pay homage to the Tron Steeple two blocks west, and the Fishmarket spire six blocks west, and the tower of St. Andrews in the Square one block west. That last of which Bonnie Prince Charlie stepped into in 1745 on the afternoon he expressed a desire to burn the entire city down for not supporting him. That first of which, the Tron, still rings its bells once a year on the birthday of Cameron of Locheil, who was granted the keys of the city for prevailing upon the Prince to spare us from flames. How inconveniently complex history really is. In the severance of self-confidence and cultural oppression after the Battle of Culloden, the Scots were made ignorant of their own history and have filled the vacuum today with shortbread, tartan candyfloss. The simplistic idea that 'Bonnie Prince Charlie' was fighting for Scottish freedom, when in fact he sought to rule all Britain and turn us all into French-speaking Catholics.

Glasgow tenements sometimes have conical or domed roofs in slate or lead above their corner bays. But *spires*, snaking segmental, polygonal gothic spires with little portholes looking to the four points of the compass: these are completely unheard of. Mine was demolished, taken away completely in the late 1970s when the building was *comprehensively rehabilitated* as the lingo of the time would have classed it, refurbished to a standard fit for contemporary living. So the spire, with all its elaborate lead sheet detailing, was deemed too expensive to put back during the re-roofing, too lavish, without function. But of course, the secret revelation, the heretical pronouncement enough to get you thrown out of the Mackintosh School of Architecture for voicing is this: that contrary to the *form follows function* maxim, everything truly brilliant in architecture is entirely without function. Show the 150-foot high black stone gothic spire of Glasgow's sexiest building: its University, to a Quantity Surveyor and he'd tell you it should have been deleted during the pre-contract cost-saving exercise. No purpose at all, silly frilly flummery and yet, and yet… how it makes the human spirit soar.

So I jokingly applied for Planning permission to put back the old spire above the flat's corner turret, then forgot about it, assuming it would get thrown out, only to discover three months later to my surprise that the Consent had been granted. I could put the spire back if I wanted to, rebuild it, scaling it from old photographs. What might I put inside it? What was inside it originally in 1870? It was probably just for show, a landmark for the bakers shop down below, the flats above for the families of those who worked all day and night baking bread and pastry in the warehouses out the back. But in my mind a new plan took shape. To turn my new spire into some kind of spiritual telescope, a lightning rod for the secret ley lines and nodal forces underpinning Glasgow's urban grid. The forces that drew medieval pilgrims back and forward along these streets still act, perhaps on the staggering junkies, drunks, the homeless, the deranged, for whom the Gallowgate seems to have a disproportionate pull.

There is no other street on earth quite like the Gallowgate. Night and day, the screams and shouts of the demented and tormented, the fixated and intoxicated, echo up from its pavements, reek like piss in its disused doorways, glitter like the broken glass of its empty car parks. People in rags, in makeshift tents, people in wheelchairs (legs amputated due to wrecking their venous system with dirty needles). Austerity Britain descends into a kind of perpetual circus-in-hell in the Gallowgate. Mad Max. Even I don't need to exaggerate it.

And then in the distance you hear the drums building, getting gradually nearer. Until the skeleton army of Ibrox come marching by, black burnt-wood rifles on their white bone shoulders, marching, marching. Only a fool would attempt to cross in front of them, especially at night, at Halloween. They come to find new recruits, among the starving, the drink-addled, the drug-crazed, the frozen, the diseased. The skeleton army of death is ever-marching, ever-expanding its roll call.

From my corner turret I gleefully toss down, one after the other, a crate-full of hand-grenades, expecting beautiful, purgative carnage. But am disappointed only a moment afterwards to see that all the scattered white bones in the moonlight know how to reassemble and re-attach themselves then just stand up and keep marching. They will be coming for me, beating on my door. Their grinning skulls pitched skyward, the black sockets of their eyes drinking all the night sky down. Here they come climbing up my stairs. I hear their bone tip-tapping on the stone steps, on the cast-iron balusters.

But it's a long way up and my door is well-bolted and lined with lead sheet, since I have long-feared this eventuality. Unless they think to go and re-group and return grinning again, ever grinning, with burning torches like the emissaries of the inferno they really are, and smoke me out or burn the whole building down. Bosch and Breughel paintings come alive, in the Gallowgate, the Gallowgate.

So ignoring the chaos I return from the window to the centre of my living room, from where I look up and then ascend into my freshly completed cosmic spire. It has a telescope at the top with which to view the moon, greatly magnified. And then a rotating one further down with which to view the three other nodal points of the Glasgow ley-line nexus, Otago Street, Queen's Park, Ibrox. Amplified enough to read the headline on a paper carried by a distant dog-walker. Like a lighthouse beam, the city is swept by my gaze, the great augmented eye of the Astronomer and Bibliophile. A spiral book-case wraps up around the spire's interior in a gently sloping helix. A retractable ladder from the living room floor pulls up into the spire base where a rotating chair for astronomical observation is counterbalanced by a second one for esoteric book reading. Room for two. Maybe Emilianna can come and join me some evening. And accompany my astral ramblings on the guitar or fiddle.

But perhaps I shouldn't have told her my theories about Ibrox. I think maybe my anger frightened her. Especially my story about how all my life I have fantasised about keeping a crate of hand-grenades by a high window ready to toss down onto the Orange-Walkers below on days when they intrude upon all the honest Saturday-morning hangovers of good people. I'm such a psycho.

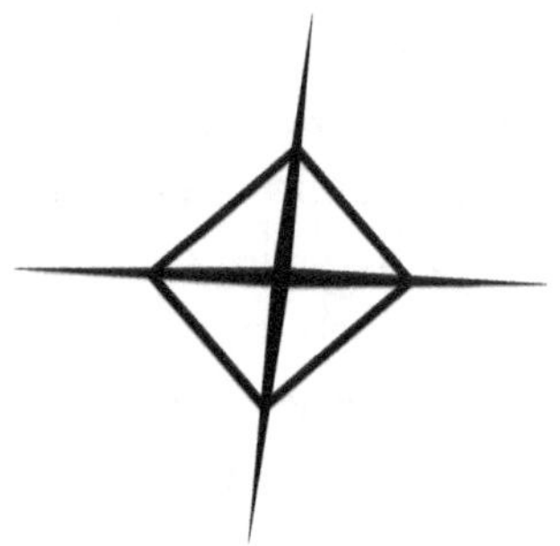

III
Emilianna

But wait. More and other late fragments of memories, sad reflections on Emilianna come flooding in, unbidden, unhidden. Although I've said that Emilianna was a Glasgow Roman Catholic of Italian descent, she was not remotely religious. Although, those things, upbringing, leave a deep mark. She and I ventured into St. Mary's Cathedral on a secret daytrip to Edinburgh one morning. November sunlight filtering down through the stained-glass windows. I was struck by how the surroundings affected her, how she lit a votive candle and placed it on the altar. I was scared to ask her what her prayer or wish was for, in case it related to me in some way. I'm such a let-down. You see, this is what I'm coming to, getting around to in these jottings, a geometrical theorem like lines drawn over a map. Connie was to me what I fear that I have become to Emilianna. Unrequited object of longing. Although at least Emilianna and I are still talking, while Connie... well, she hates me these days more than anything in the universe apparently, so I'm told. I am anathema, anti-Christ to her very existence. But by not loving Emilianna back I gain an understanding of what it's like for Connie to not love me back. You see? Am I cruel, too abstract, insane? It's about closing a circle, or a triangle, or a square, healing the wound, or perhaps one of many, inherent in the Creator's flawed plan for the mechanics of human attraction.

Where was I, where am I? Emilianna has black hair and dark eyes, a pretty face shaped like a heart, a deeply endearing smile. A profoundly-held optimism, a steady practical regard for life, a hug that could crush you, surprisingly strong arms. Probably something to do with having raised two sons, of course. Housewives bearing babes in the crook of their elbows while negotiating domestic chores quickly develop biceps worthy of east-European athletes of the soviet era. Emilianna is a survivor, tough enough not to let a failed love-affair with me knock her psychologically off-course. Unlike Connie of course, whose madness attracted me, whose madness repelled herself from me… leaving me… forlorn. Half mad myself, arguably.

Later that morning we strolled through Dean cemetery on its high plateau above a bend in the Water of Leith (so like the sweet waters of Lethe of Greek myth in the forgetful fields of Elysium). In gentle autumn sunlight, kicked among the yellow leaves of faded time, we found ourselves surprisingly alone, shivered at the place, a kind of Scottish Père Lachaise. We walked down into the dense wooded glades of Dean Village afterwards, and on a particularly steep cobbled hill she took my hand. Then did not want to let go for several hundred yards afterwards. It was nothing to do with the slope or the surface, I fear. She had fallen in love with me, or something approaching it. What damage have I done? Just as Connie did to me? This triangle, squared with evil, is in fact the circle of God's laughing mouth. *La Ronde.* Round and around the cycle of human attraction goes, with everybody missing the point and the goal of their desires, everyone going hungry and thirsty. Nobody satisfied. Everyone deceived. Humankind, what cure is there for your ailment of desire? Except to put you all in one big bed together one day at the end of time and then… well, what? Isn't a quiet chat and a hug and a sleep afterwards always the best of it anyway? Death the sleep and earth the bed then. We'll just have to make do.

On the way back on the train, I drew her portrait in my sketchbook and wrote her what almost felt like a final poem:

> Drawing you is as if
> for a moment my hand
> becomes the hand of Gaia
> better hands than these hands
> hands that caress your hair
> trace the curve of your cheek
> the dimple of your chin

soft lines of your brow
each exquisite note of the melody
of the beauty of your face
hands of the father
hands of an absent creator
touch of infinite softness, lightness
touch of admiration, never trespass
owning nothing, accepting all
hands of greeting and farewell
my fingers tracing your perfection
enact the opposite of creation
unmaking of authorship:

they set you free.

But it wasn't the last poem. I still occasionally write others to her, for her. We stay in touch and meet perhaps once every couple of months. Our penances, our hair-shirts worked. My six months stripping and painting at Gallowgate, her applying for various full-time administrative jobs, one of which eventually suited her and she stuck with. Reasonable pay and conditions, not too demanding, nor too dull. Working for Glasgow's public transport executive, strangely enough. I meant to say something about trains, past and present.

Having grown up here I have been blind to so much, taken too much for granted and at face value. It's taken me almost half a century to realise that we in Glasgow and Scotland have spent our entire lives inside an enormous recession, relative to the prosperity of the Victorian era. We were once, famously, the 'second city of the British Empire', building boats and trains, trading in sugar and tobacco, profiting from slavery and all the other myriad evils of empire. The tangible legacy of that is about two square miles of some of the finest Victorian office buildings in Britain, if not the world. They drip with statuary, of heroes and gods and angels borrowed from antiquity, aligning Glasgow with Athens and Rome and Florence, as the inheritor of the lineage of classical enlightenment. But there is also the incredible feats of engineering. The stations, the bridges, the tunnels. Of the latter, so many are disused and forgotten now, but still there. The inner city population dropped dramatically in the 1960s, and has never really recovered since, as vast areas of unsanitary slum housing were demolished and families moved out to suburbia. The city's grey industrial lungs have coughed to a halt, fractured and contracted, grown cold. The empty railway tunnels, silent save for the dripping of water and the scuttle of rats, are its veins and arteries, criss-crossing the city, the wires of a corroded battery, a hardened old heart. But being inorganic of course, it is intrinsically immortal, cannot rot. Like the ley lines, the culverted streams, the lost routes once walked by pilgrims, this network meshes, acts as a dream-amplifier, a reservoir of post-industrial romance. The sweet melancholy of Glasgow exudes from its hidden strength beneath its moss, its rust, its dusty, scaled and cracking skin.

And so I have wandered over and across and through these inhabited ruins we call a city, with Connie and Emilianna and all the other lost lovers, their names tarnished or turning into gold, as souvenirs. Like ants across a fallen carcass, we have scarcely understood the ailing beast which has sustained us, even as we shivered in the chill breeze of its dying breaths.

A year has nearly gone by now since Emilianna and I first *fell in*. The madness has passed. Our lives are saner and perhaps just a little dull. As with Connie, I miss the fire but not the terror. I am resolved to live a straighter and more decent life. I have never stopped loving my wife, who deserves better than me and all this insanity. But I have resolved to try to become that better person. It's not my loins that are the problem, I'd swear it. It is my heart, which is too open, too full, too overflowing. In that sense I would love everyone if I could, but our society forbids such transgression.

When my mother died, her old upright piano was left homeless as it were, no room for it in my suburban bungalow, and so by various detours it found its way to my eccentric office space. It was where Emilianna and I first rehearsed together, one summer afternoon when she brought her violin over, while my employers were away on holiday. These days I sometimes play it when I first arrive in the morning, alone with my thoughts, gazing over its dark polished wood top to the view through the draughty warehouse windows of the sun coming up over Glasgow. It is magnificently out of tune, but characterful.

This summer the trees have grown so high
I can no longer see your window
across the Kelvin across the abandoned rail yard
over the husk of industrial urban memory
echo footstep culture imprint fossil
where the cars park and pay-and-display
their tickets to forgetful utopias
indefinitely postponed on disused land

And when I play the piano at daybreak
and my music drifts across the waste
of No Man's Land unlike last summer
I know you're not even there to strain
to hear but left for work already seeking
solace of penance these hair shirts
we've woven and worn, the good slaves
that pace the exercise yard of voluntary arrest

And so we stopped, we stopped
The moon tonight is glowing
perfect half until binoculars confirm
its pocked white surface and skull face
it's all dead really.
The light is our own.

IV
Black Cormorant

I am Emilianna Verrecchio. I make this statement of my own freewill. I killed Douglas Thompson. I hereby confess to the crime, Officer. I stuck my Italian grandfather's antique stiletto blade into his heart because he had bewitched and hypnotised me somehow, stolen my past, made me believe that I was his lost lover Connie. When and how did he bring this change about? Was it when he first walked me through what we talked about as a time portal in Queen's Park? I thought it was all a joke, a crazy harmless fantasy of his. Was it really something more? Some kind of sorcery? The man was a dark angel, a demon, spawn of the devil, that's for sure, and I did the world a favour by ridding it of him and his foul influence.

Not at first did I notice any change, but it came slowly, gradually in the days after by small degrees. My memory grew hazy in unexpected areas, specific places, as if holes were forming, like snow melting in spring or...

(tape becomes unintelligible).

I wanted to know who Connie had really been.
How she had really died. I had begun my own
investigations behind Douglas's back and…

One time I phoned her apartment and
caught her in. We spoke briefly on the phone but
by the time I'd ran out and jumped into a taxi
and sped round to her neighbourhood, she had
fled apparently, only minutes before. What did
she sound like? Normal, nothing extraordinary.
Oddly familiar. A bit like, a bit like… No, but
that would make no sense. You think I'm mad,
don't you? But I'm not. Connie was alive, had
never died. I should have been relieved because
this proved that Douglas was no murderer. And
yet… I still needed to see her in person I felt, to
actually touch her. But as I've said, something was
going wrong, gradually, with my memory. Did
I have lead poisoning, the early stages of a brain
tumour? Apparently not, as your own medics will
have confirmed in custody. Yes? I thought so. Well,
that's a relief of sorts I suppose. Or is it? Just so I
can enjoy every second of the next thirty years in
prison in exquisite detail? Did I ever find Connie,
meet her face to face? Why are you smirking? You
do think I'm mad, don't you? Oh I saw her one
night alright, after my thousandth attempt, in the
thick fog down by the banks of the Kelvin, a few

hundred feet from my own flat. She was laughing with a couple of friends, and I cried out to her, called her by name. She turned and saw me and dropped a glass of red wine she was holding in her hand, which then exploded on the wet cobbles at her feet. And then…

Then what? The look on her face, I'll never forget it, of wonder, of fear, of having been found out for something, tracked down and pinned down like some kind of wild animal, a fabulous butterfly! What then? Why, I watched her outline growing darker and darker over a few seconds, her friends peeling away like illusory husks of some discarded pupa. Her eyes grew red, fiery red and large. Her hair and coat grew feathery and spiky. Connie transformed into a black cormorant, tall and thin and oily. Sinister, with a long lethal beak, skeletal legs, a peculiar gait and way of strutting and bounding. They spread their black wings like a huge umbrella, you know, it's what they're famous for, just before they kill. It's so they can throw a shadow over the still water of a river and see the fish down below once they're removed the sheen of glimmer from the sun-bright surface. And so it was. I thought for a moment she was going to kill me, skewer me through the heart with her sharp beak as she reared up and blotted out the moon and stars behind her with her umbrella fan of black feathers. She made some weird final hissing and croaking sound and then bang! She was gone just like that. They move so fast when they decide to, finally, after all that patience and hanging around. I think I saw her plunge into the river, or perhaps spread her wings wide and lift off into the night. But she was gone suddenly, and I was alone again. Almost as alone as I feel now.

After that I lost my way, forgot my name, for several days and nights, wandered in a trance, a dwam, until I walked into that lecture room that night to hear Douglas Thompson read aloud his new collection of poetry, which seemed to me to make sense of everything. And then for a moment it seemed as if I knew who I was again, who he was, and why I had to kill him. Because our fates had been, and always will be, forever intertwined. He had a wife who loves and mourns him, you say? Well, that wouldn't surprise me at all now, would it? My name is Emilianna after all, and the name means 'rival'. Douglas chose it, gave it to me, he created me out of nothing, out of fog pouring off the River Kelvin, and writers often place great significance in names. It's one of those things, one of many things, that readers ought to be on guard for. But they never are, and never learn, just like the rest of us.

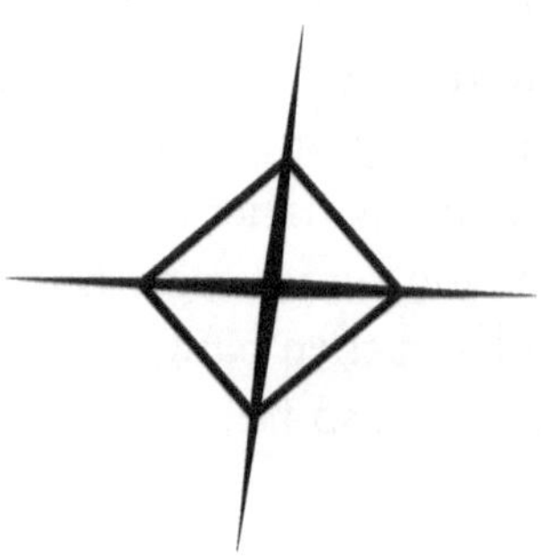

V
The Fifth Point

All of the foregoing text, including that purporting to be written by Douglas Thompson, was in fact written and dictated by one Emilianna Verrechio, who has today been sectioned under the Mental Health Act in the presence of two witnesses and committed to a secure institution to be detained indefinitely. To our knowledge, no significant Glasgwegian writer called Douglas Thompson has ever existed, and thus Ms Verrechio has in fact neither killed, nor done harm to, anyone.

Who dreamt who? Perhaps we all dream each other. Or perhaps falling in love is the moment at which we begin to dream another person, and by the virtue of that dreaming, from that very moment forward, begin to murder and erase the real person who is increasingly obscured beneath the accruing, increasingly deceptive layers, of our love for them.

Perhaps therefore most of us spend the majority of our lives wrapped like moths or caterpillars in numb cocoons of other people's love and expectations for us. And we are supposed to be the lucky ones. But maybe the lonely, the truly free and alone, are the only brief butterflies, who get to break out beyond the straitjacket of suffocating social convention, and flicker upwards into the burning, bright blue sky. O Picaresque Icarus. May you ever avoid the insidious stilettos, the pins of the librarian lapidarians, the lepidopterists. Flicker, flitter, flutter on.

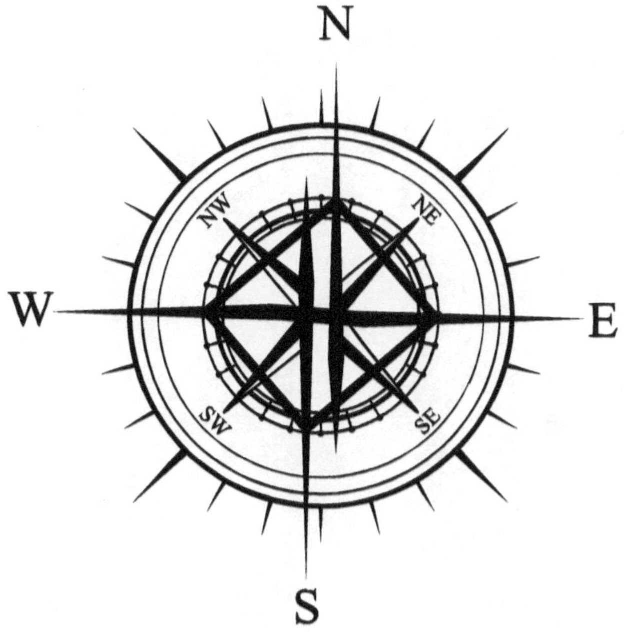

N
NW
NE
W
E
SW
SE
S

www.ingramcontent.com/pod-product-compliance
Lightning Source LLC
Chambersburg PA
CBHW031419200726
48285CB00017BA/2565